MY FIRST
I Can Read Book®

I See, You Saw

written and illustrated by
Nurit Karlin

HarperCollinsPublishers

I See, You Saw

For information address HarperCollins Children's
Books, a division of HarperCollins Publishers,
195 Broadway, New York, NY 10007.

Library of Congress Cataloging-in-Publication Data
Karlin, Nurit.
I see, you saw / by Nurit Karlin.
p. cm. — (My first I can read book)
Summary: Two cats take a stroll and find a seesaw, which one of them saws.
ISBN 0-06-026677-5. — ISBN 0-06-026678-3 (lib. bdg.)
ISBN 0-06-444249-7 (pbk.)
[1. Cats—Fiction.] I. Title. II. Series.
PZ7.K1424Iaaj 1997 96-27261
[E]—dc20 CIP
AC

First Harper Trophy edition, 1999
19 20 LSCC 30 29 28 27
❖
Visit us on the World Wide Web!
http://www.harperchildrens.com

I See, You Saw

"Look! A can!"

“I see the can.

“I can kick the can.”

"I see a fly.

"I can see the fly fly."

"Look!"

"A seesaw!"

"We can seesaw."

"I see, you saw."

"No. I see, *you* saw.

"I saw the seesaw first!"

"I see a bee."

"I saw the bee."

"I see the sea."

"Look! A saw!"

"I can see the saw."

"I can saw the seesaw."

"Stop! Look up!"

"Where?" "There!"

“It is coming down!”

“Quick! Duck!”

Quack

Quack

"It is a duck."

“I see the duck.”

“I see a fish.”

“I saw the duck fish the fish.”

"I saw *you* duck the duck."

"And *I* saw *you*
saw the seesaw."